Wheels and Axles

Siân Smith

Heinemann
LIBRARY

Chicago, Illinois

www.capstonepub.com
Visit our website to find out more information about Heinemann-Raintree books.

To order:
☎ Phone 800-747-4992
💻 Visit www.capstonepub.com to browse our catalog and order online.

© 2012 Heinemann Library
an imprint of Capstone Global Library, LLC
Chicago, Illinois

Edited by Dan Nunn, Rebecca Rissman, and Sian Smith
Designed by Joanna Hinton-Malivoire
Picture research by Mica Brancic
Production by Victoria Fitzgerald

Originated by Capstone Global Library Ltd
Printed and bound in China by South China Printing Company Ltd

16 15 14 13 12
10 9 8 7 6 5 4 3 2 1

Library of Congress Cataloging-in-Publication Data

Smith, Siân.
  Wheels and axles / Siân Smith.
    p. cm.—(How toys work)
  Includes bibliographical references and index.
  ISBN 978-1-4329-6584-6 (hb)—ISBN 978-1-4329-6591-4 (pb)
1. Wheels—Juvenile literature. 2. Axles—Juvenile literature. 3. Toys—Juvenile literature. I. Title.
  TJ181.5.S58 2013
  621.8'23—dc23   2011041313

Acknowledgments

The author and publisher are grateful to the following for permission to reproduce copyright material: © Capstone Global Library Ltd pp.7 (Tudor Photography), 11 bottom (Lord and Leverett); © Capstone Publishers pp.5, 8, 9, 18, 12 inset, 12 main, 13 inset, 13 main, 23 top (Karon Dubke); Shutterstock pp. 4 bottom left (© Kellis), 4 bottom right (© Studio Smart), 4 top left (© Mikeledray), 4 top right (© Jamalludin), 6 (© Zurijeta), 10 bottom (© Martin Allinger), 10 top (© charles taylor), 11 top (© Oriori), 15 (© Mika Heittola), 16 (© Alexander Sakhatovsky), 17 (© Pixel1962), 19 (© Greenland), 20 (© Losevsky Pavel), 21 (© Rupena), 22a (© Martin Plsek), 22b (© Vlue), 22d (© Chepe Nicoli), 22d (© Jakub Krechowicz), 23 bottom (© Alexander Sakhatovsky).

Cover photograph of a boy on a bicycle reproduced with permission of Getty Images (altrendo images/Altrendo). Back cover photograph of a scooter reproduced with permission of Shutterstock (© Greenland).

We would like to thank Nancy Harris, Dee Reid, and Diana Bentley for their assistance in the preparation of this book.

Every effort has been made to contact copyright holders of material reproduced in this book. Any omissions will be rectified in subsequent printings if notice is given to the publisher.

All the Internet addresses (URLs) given in this book were valid at the time of going to press. However, due to the dynamic nature of the Internet, some addresses may have changed, or sites may have changed or ceased to exist since publication. While the author and publisher regret any inconvenience this may cause readers, no responsibility for any such changes can be accepted by either the author or the publisher.

Contents

Different Toys 4

Wheels 6

Axles. 12

Moving Toys 16

Quiz 22

Picture Glossary. 23

Index .24

Different Toys

There are many different kinds of toys.

Toys work in different ways.

Wheels

wheel

Some toys move on wheels.

A go-kart moves on wheels.

Toys move when they are pushed
or pulled.

Toys with wheels are easier to move.

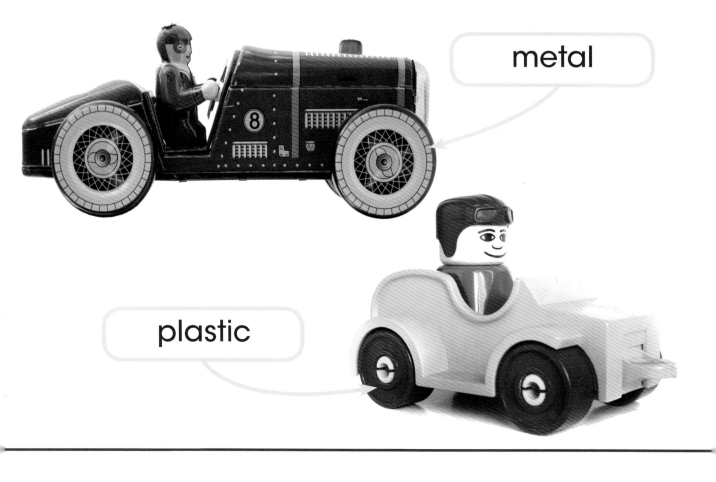

metal

plastic

Toy wheels can be made of metal or plastic.

wood

rubber

Toy wheels can be made of wood
or rubber.

Axles

axle

An axle is like a rod.

axle

Some axles stay still. Wheels move around on them.

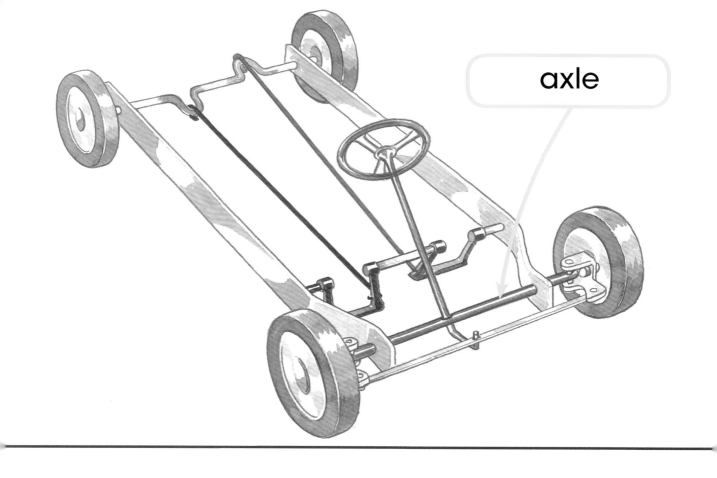

axle

Some wheels are stuck on axles.

When the axle moves, the wheels move, too.

Moving Toys

Electricity can make some things move.

Electricity makes the wheels on this race car move.

Water makes some toy wheels move.

Pushes from people make some toy wheels move.

A merry-go-round is a wheel you can push.

Roller skates have wheels you can push.

Quiz

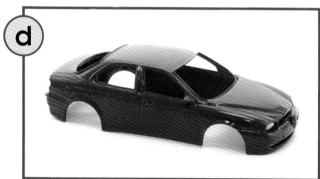

Which one of these toys is missing its wheels?

Answer on page 24

Picture Glossary

 **axle** rod that has a wheel at each end

 **electricity** electricity can be used to make some things move. There is a small amount of electricity in batteries.

Index

axle 12–15

go-kart 7

merry-go-round 20

pull 8

push 8, 19, 20, 21

roller skates 21

Answer to question on page 22: Toy d is missing its wheels.

Notes for Parents and Teachers
Introduction
Show the children a collection of toys. One or more of the toys should have wheels. Ask the children if they can spot the toy or toys with wheels. Do they know what an axle is? Why do we use wheels?

More information about wheels and axles
Explain that we use wheels to make things easier to move. You could demonstrate this by pushing a toy car with wheels, as well as one without. Show the children a good example of two wheels on an axle. Explain that an axle is like a bar or rod, and that a wheel is put on each end of the axle. Some axles are fixed in place, and the wheels are free to move around on them. Other axles are free to move, but the wheels are fixed in place, and when the axle turns or moves, the wheels move, too.

Follow-up activities
Tell the children that there are five wheels on page 14. Can they see the fifth wheel? Explain that a steering wheel is an example of a wheel on an axle, too. Ask the children to sort toys or pictures of toys based on the type of material the toy wheels are made from. For more advanced work on simple machines, children can work with an adult to discuss and play the games at: www.edheads.org/activities/simple-machines.

24